THE WONDERFUL

DAHLOV IPCAR

EGG

FLYING EYE BOOKS

Alex Spiro and Sam Arthur would like to thank Robert Ipcar for his invaluable assistance with this project and Dahlov Ipcar for her beautiful words and pictures and for the honour to introduce them to a new generation of children.

We would also like to thank the Nobrow design team for their meticulous labour on the restoration of the artwork to its original form.

This is a first Flying Eye Books edition.
The Wonderful Egg is © 2014 Flying Eye Books.
First published by Doubleday & Company, Inc. in 1958.

ISBN 978-1-909263-28-4
Order from www.flyingeyebooks.com

For Bobby, who wanted dinosaur pictures

In the back of this book, you will find a chart that tells you how big the dinosaurs were, and a page that tells you how to say their names.

Long, long, long ago, more than one hundred million years ago, everything was different than it is today. It was so long ago that there were no cities or houses or even people. All the earth was covered with big green jungles. They were hot, damp, tangled jungles of huge moss trees and giant fern trees. For even the trees were different then.

Back in those long-ago times, the only animals that lived in the green jungles of the world were the dinosaurs. They were very strange beasts and most of them were big. Stupendously, tremendously, enormously BIG.

They trampled through the green jungles on their big feet, and they waded through the swamps. Other huge reptiles swam in the warm seas. Some even flew through the air on big leather bat-wings. And they all laid eggs.

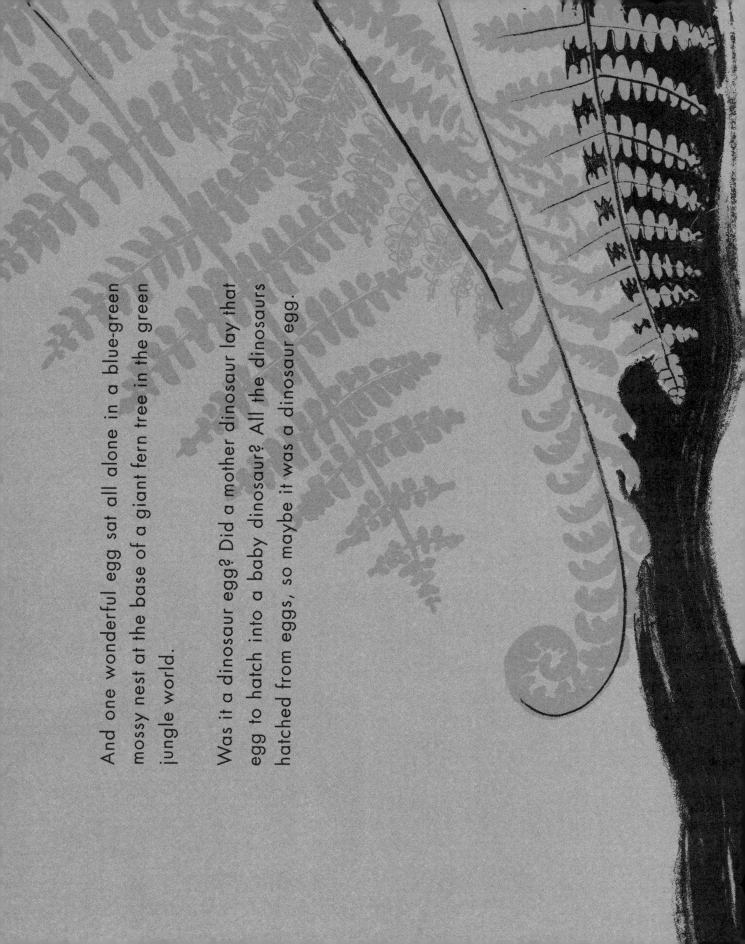

And one wonderful egg sat all alone in a blue-green mossy nest at the base of a giant fern tree in the green jungle world.

Was it a dinosaur egg? Did a mother dinosaur lay that egg to hatch into a baby dinosaur? All the dinosaurs hatched from eggs, so maybe it was a dinosaur egg.

Was it a Brontosaurus egg? Brontosaurus was a really ENORMOUS dinosaur, the huge "thunder-lizard". He had a great heavy body on thick legs like tree trunks, a long trailing tail, and a long snake-like neck with a little head like a salamander's head, looking this way and that, swaying along, wading through the green marshy swamps of long ago.

Was it a Triceratops egg? Triceratops was big, too, but not as big as Brontosaurus. He had two big horns over his eyes and another horn on his hooked beak of a nose, and he had a big bony frill around his neck. There were several kinds of big dinosaurs with horns and frills, but Triceratops was the biggest.

Or was it a Stegosaurus egg? Stegosaurus was big, too. He had rows of high bony plates that ran up and down his back like a fence all the way to the tip of his long tail, and at the end of his tail he had four big spikes.

Pteranodon was a huge flying reptile with great wings like a bat, more than twenty feet across from tip to tip. He flew high over the green treetops on his big flapping wings. Perhaps it was a Pteranodon egg?

Maybe it was an Ornithomimus egg? Ornithomimus, the "ostrich dinosaur", was timid and he could run very fast. He had a beak like a bird's and a long neck, and he walked on his hind legs. He looked almost like a long-tailed featherless ostrich.

Or was it an Elasmosaurus egg? Elasmosaurus was one of the big reptiles that lived in the deep seas of long ago. He was one of the biggest, sometimes measuring forty feet from the tip of his nose to the tip of his tail. He swam and dived in the water and had four flippers like a seal, but he had a long neck like a snake, and a short snake-like tail.

Could it be a Tyrannosaurus egg? Tyrannosaurus was the largest of the big hunting dinosaurs. He was very ferocious, with terrible teeth, and he hunted and ate other dinosaurs. He walked upright on his strong heavy hind legs, and the earth shook under him as he stalked through the jungles on his big clawed feet looking for his prey.

Trachodon was another big dinosaur that walked on his hind legs, but he was gentle and peaceful and ate plants. He had a narrow, flat head with a nose shaped like a duck's bill. He lived in the swamplands, where he splashed in the mud and swam in the water. Perhaps it was a Trachodon egg?

Or was it a Corythosaurus egg? Corythosaurus was another duck-billed dinosaur that liked to swim and wade in the swamps. He was the "helmet-crested" duck-bill.

Parasaurolophus was duck-billed, too, but with a different kind of crest on his head. Could it be a Parasaurolophus egg?

Tylosaurus was another big reptile that lived in the warm seas. He had four flippers, and perhaps a wavy fin down his back and along his tail. And he had a big mouth full of sharp teeth for catching fish. Was it a Tylosaurus egg?

Or could it be an Ankylosaurus egg? Ankylosaurus was a medium-sized dinosaur with thick, armor-like plates of bone all over his back and big spikes sticking out all along his sides.

But no, it wasn't a dinosaur egg at all.

It was a wonderful new kind of egg.

And when it hatched, it hatched into a baby bird, the first baby bird in the whole world. And the baby bird grew up to be a beautiful bird with feathers. The first beautiful bird that ever sang a song high in the treetops of the green world of long, long ago.

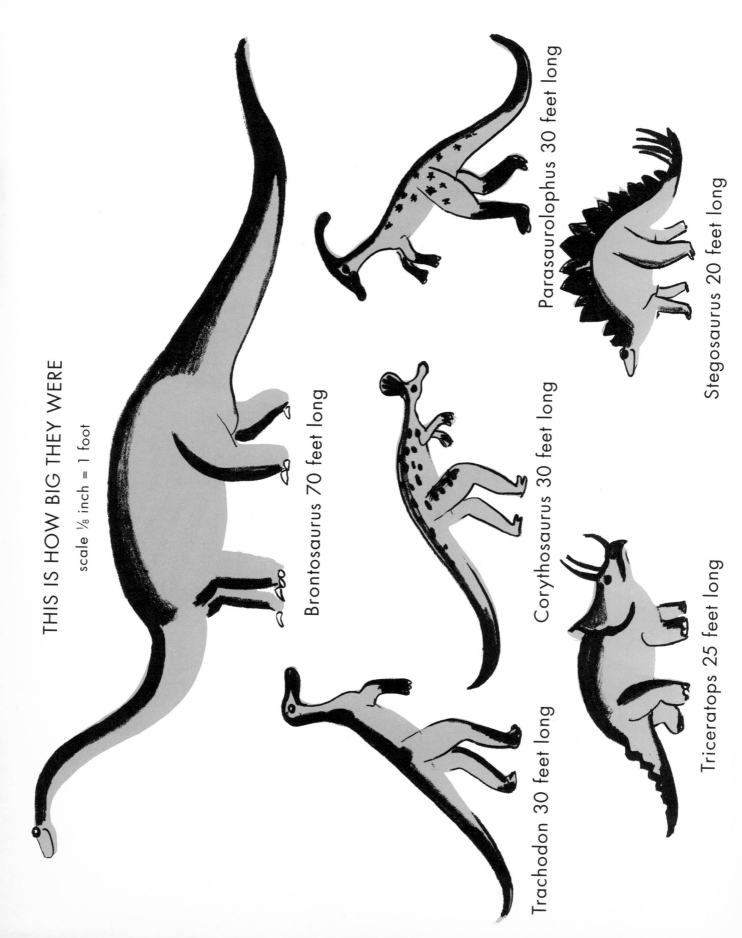

THIS IS HOW BIG THEY WERE

scale ⅛ inch = 1 foot

Brontosaurus 70 feet long

Parasaurolophus 30 feet long

Stegosaurus 20 feet long

Corythosaurus 30 feet long

Trachodon 30 feet long

Triceratops 25 feet long

Ornithomimus 12 feet long

Ankylosaurus 10 feet long

Tylosaurus 30 feet long

Tyrannosaurus 50 feet long

Pteranodon 25-foot wingspread

Elasmosaurus 40 feet long

Rhamphorhynchus
(small flying reptile)

Archaeopteryx
(the first bird)

Both chicken-sized

THIS IS THE WAY TO SAY THEIR NAMES

Ankylosaurus   AN-kill-o-sawr-us

Archaeopteryx   ark-e-OP-teri-ix

Brontosaurus   BRON-toe-sawr-us

Corythosaurus   cor-ITH-o-sawr-us

Elasmosaurus   ee-LAZ-mo-sawr-us

Ornithomimus   orn-i-tho-MYME-us

Parasaurolophus   pear-a-sawr-OL-o-fus

Pteranodon   tare-AN-o-don

Rhamphorhynchus   ram-fo-RINK-us

Stegosaurus   STEG-o-sawr-us

Trachodon   TRACK-o-don

Triceratops   try-SER-a-tops

Tylosaurus   TILE-o-sawr-us

Tyrannosaurus   tie-RAN-o-sawr-us

Rhamphorhynchus

Archaeopteryx